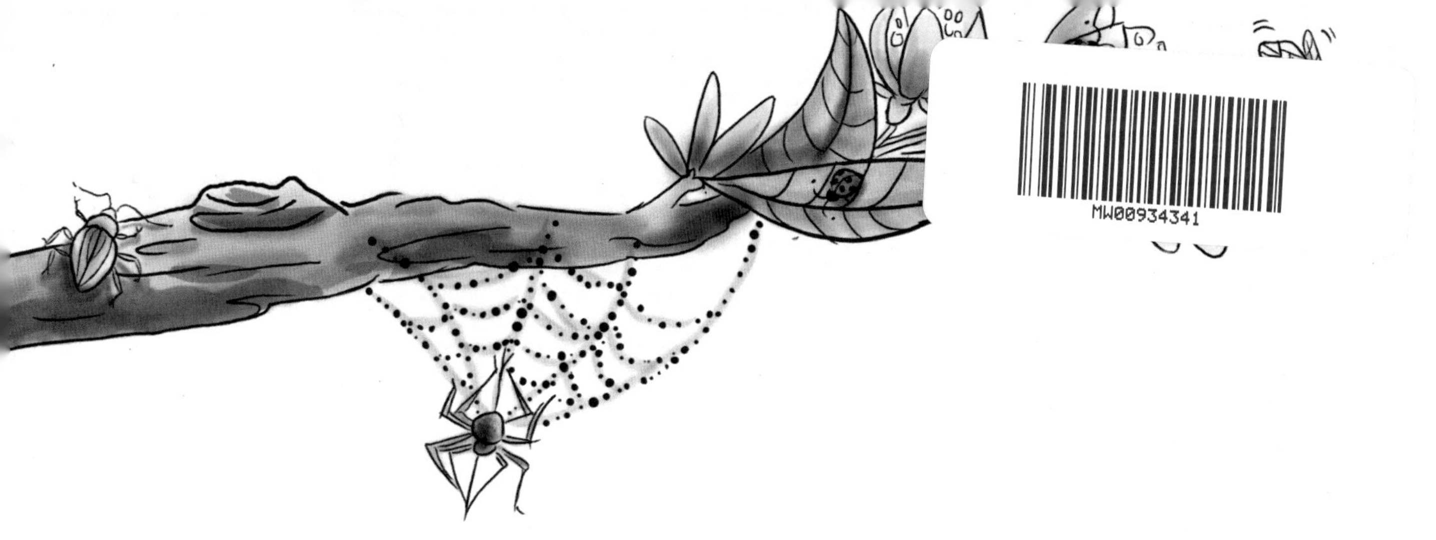



# THE DRAB CATERPILLAR

by Majo

Illustrated by Adrienne Brown

This is the story of a drab caterpillar. You know, she was one of those brownish colored ones… you look at her but don't really see her. Most of her life, she just crawled along only looking down.

During the day, she was unaware of the beautiful sun in all its glory. At night, she never noticed the man in the moon as he illuminated the star-studded sky.

The drab caterpillar had always been told, “You aren’t as pretty as the other caterpillars. You’re too plain and too plump. You probably won’t amount to much, but that’s okay. There are lots of things you can do…even though they aren’t glamorous or exciting.”

Drab loved to sing, but never loud enough for others to hear her. She was sure her voice was dull and mediocre just like the rest of her. Singing always made her feel joyful. At times, she would imagine herself a big star, with others clamoring to be near her and to love her.

One day, while climbing up a very large willow tree, Drab glimpsed the Sun peeping through the swaying branches. Without any warning, her heart burst into a sweet sounding song. The Sun, nestled comfortably in the azure sky, smiled warmly down on the drab caterpillar. “I enjoyed your singing,” she beamed.

Embarrassed, Drab tried to hide from the dazzling Sun's view.

"Where'd you go?" teased the Sun.

The drab caterpillar peeked out from the rustling leaves. "Something amazing just happened," she stammered. Shyly, she told the smiling Sun of her new discovery.

“When I looked up and saw you, all of a sudden my heart seemed to burst open with joy.  I couldn’t control myself,” stuttered the caterpillar breathlessly.

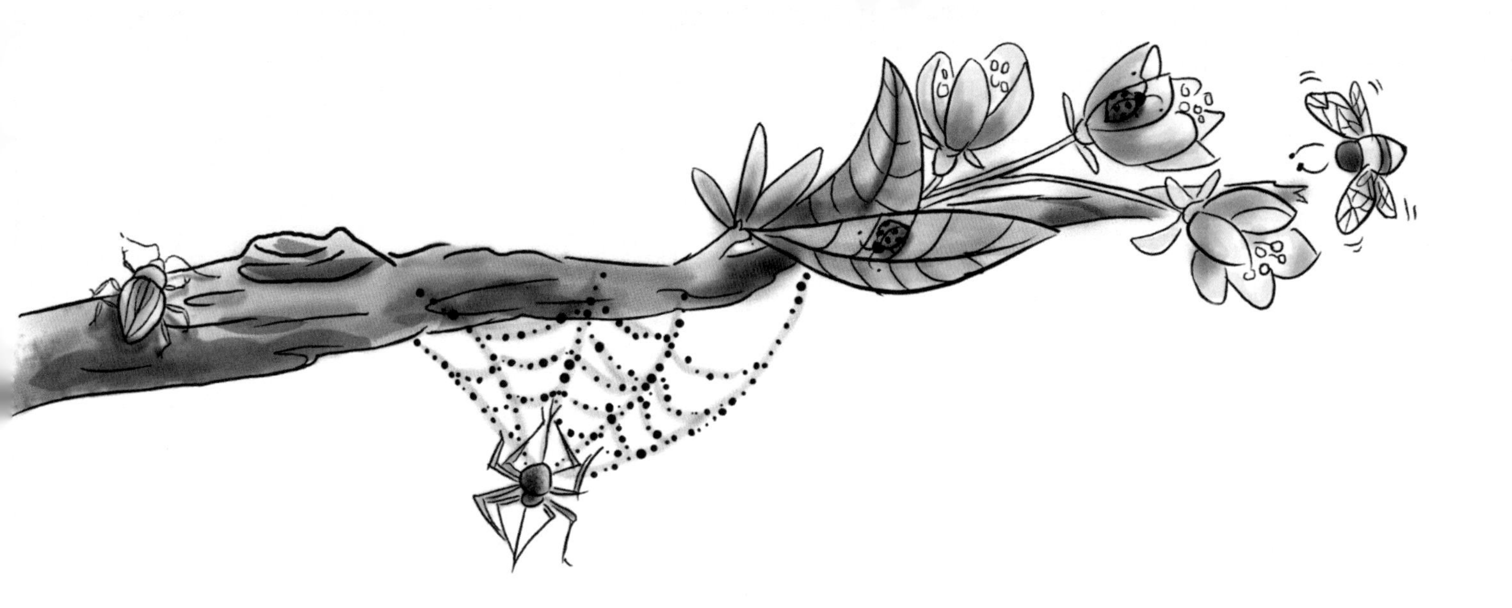

"At last!" radiated the Sun. "I've been coaxing you for so long to look up. You, on the other hand, insisted on looking down."

"Wow! But now I can see for myself," she answered excitedly. " It's amazing!... It's marvelous!… And you know what? I'm beginning to smell the blossoms on this tree. They're awesome!"

"There is so much more in store for you," smiled the Sun. "I will show you how to be beautiful."

"Beautiful!!! Why, I'll never be beautiful," Drab cried out with amazement.

"I think you are already beautiful," said the Sun. "There is much more to you than you think. Come on… follow me… you'll see."

"No!" said the caterpillar stubbornly. "I don't want to. I'm afraid. I've always been drab. I'm actually quite comfortable the way I am."

"Humph!!…comfortable," the Sun retorted. "But are you free?… Can you fly?"

"Fly! You're joking! I can hardly even crawl," the drab caterpillar chuckled.

“You were never meant to crawl forever,” the Sun replied tenderly. “You were born to fly. Soon you’ll spread your wings to their fullest and sing your song to the world.”

“Are you kidding me!” the caterpillar said laughingly. “If you haven’t noticed, I don’t have any wings. Sing my song! That’s a joke. Who would listen to my singing anyway?”

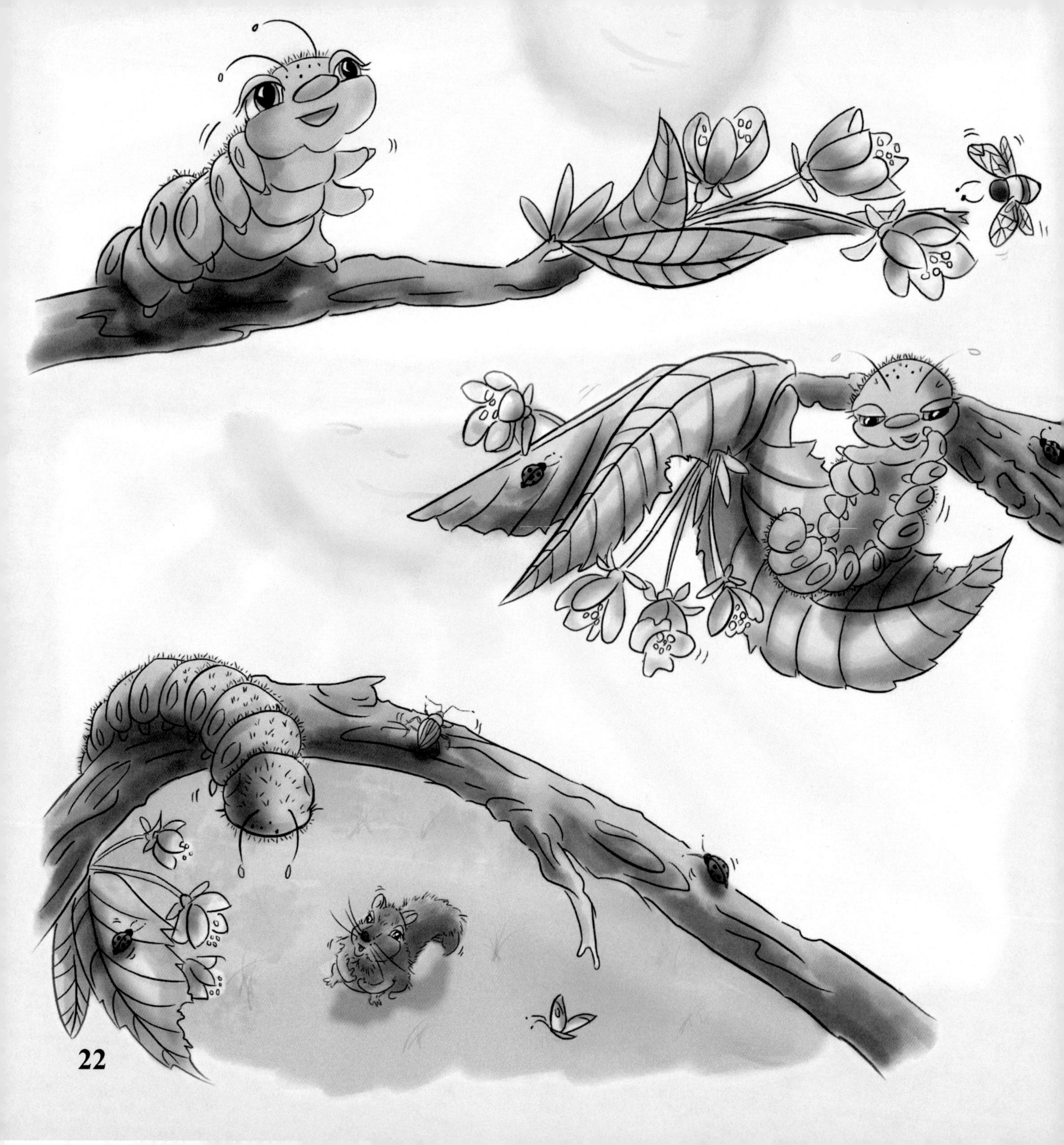

“It doesn’t matter who listens! What is important is that you sing your song,” encouraged the Sun.

“Others will laugh at me,” the caterpillar whispered.

“Let them laugh. Who cares,” the Sun said warmly.

“I care!!” Drab yelled. “It hurts my heart!! Bland as I am, I still have feelings.”

"No one likes to be laughed at," said the Sun gently. "But you will have wings… and can fly away from their laughter."

"What's all this talk about flying?" said the flabbergasted caterpillar. "I keep telling you…all I do is climb around this tree all day and eat leaves."

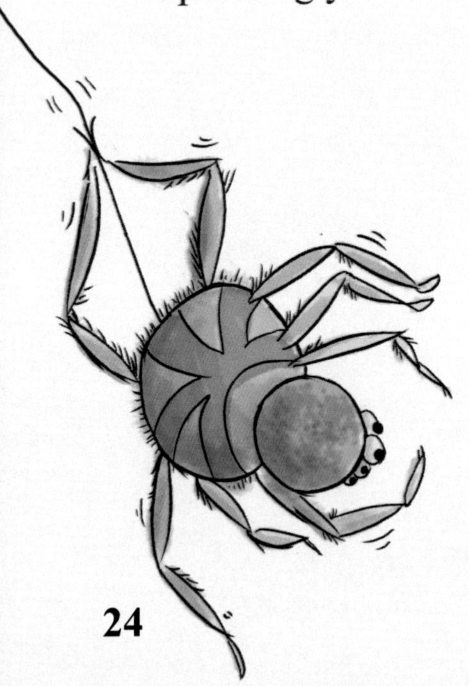

"You will see a very beautiful world, if you follow me," said the Sun brilliantly. "I guarantee that someday you will learn to fly. You'll glide from flower to flower, drinking in their nectar. You'll skim along the clear blue ponds. Maybe, you'll even have a friend or two."

"Wow!  It sounds like fun," Drab said excitedly.  "Sure, I've had some wild dreams of a different life.  I wished I were famous and all that.  But I'm kind of used to being a drab caterpillar.  And, it sounds risky.  Hey, with all that talk of flying… I might even die."

The Sun smiled down on the drab caterpillar tenderly. “In some ways, we all have to die…in order to be reborn… so to speak.”

“Yeah, well…that sounds pretty scary. I think I’ll take a pass. I’ll just stay the way I am.”

“Then, you’ll never be free, and you’ll never fly…. Is that what you want?” asked the Sun.

“Not really. But you make it sound too easy… like I’ll never get hurt,” the caterpillar replied.

The bright yellow Sun thought for a moment. “Whenever we decide to make some changes, it probably will hurt a little. Pain is a necessary part of growing. But trust me… the joy you will feel, will make it all worthwhile.”

“Do you think you could help me?” Drab pleaded.

“Of course,” exclaimed the Sun. “I’ll always be with you. As a matter of fact, I’ll even light your way.”

“Gee whiz,” said the drab caterpillar astonished. “I’d really like to fly. I’d love to sing…REALLY, REALLY LOUD!!! Smelling the beautiful flowers would be amazing….When do we start?”

“I think you’ve already started,” said the setting Sun. “Now come on. Let’s get going. And remember…KEEP LOOKING UP!!! There’s nothing down there that you haven’t seen before.”

*The End*

*or is it*

*The Beginning*

# Illustrator

Adrienne Brown was born and raised in Kansas. "So early on in my childhood I was amazed by sketching and doodling". I absolutely loved picture books. As I grew up I collected all I could. I longed to be a children's book illustrator." Most of her career was in graphic design and illustration. "You name it, I have probably drawn it."

She now resides in the Mountains of Idaho with her husband and daughter. Snuggled in the mountains and illustrating as much as possible. "I love the personal collaboration with Majo and creating her characters. Helping her wonderful stories come to life is an incredible feeling. I am truly blessed to be a part of it all."

Contact Adrienne at adbrown14@gmail.com or papermoonco.com

# Author Biography

Majo is a wife, mother, grandmother, writer and entrepreneur who promotes positive thinking, and achieving a high quality of life. While raising her family, she began her career as a corporate consultant, training employees in team building, sales and diversity. She also earned a real estate license, wrote a column called "The Family Hour" for a Philadelphia area newspaper and modeled in print and television. She founded three businesses to foster personal accountability, successful parenting and improving the prevalent cultural mindset regarding women in advertising.

Of all her many accomplishments, Majo is most proud of being the Mother of her eight children and grandmother of many. Majo is a beautiful, energetic and determined entrepreneur. She has written six books for children as well as adults, HUMBLE PIE, THE COOL CHAMELEON, CLEO THE COLD FISH, LESSONS ON FLYING, A DOG AND CAT RELATIONSHIP, and THE DRAB CATTERPILLAR. It has taken her 30 years and many, many rejection letters to achieve this goal. The saying "It's never too late" and Bob Dylan's quote "He who is not busy being born, is busy dying" motivate Majo to keep growing.

Majo is married and lives in Doylestown, PA.

Contact Majo at her website:
MajoTheAuthor.com or email: mjbgd@aol.com

Made in the USA
Middletown, DE
22 December 2021